AF417492

Our Lives

WITH THE

Boys Band

BRANDI MIQUELE

MILTON & HUGO L.L.C.
1001 3rd Avenue West, Suite 430
Bradenton, FL 34205, USA

Website: *www. miltonandhugo.com*
Hotline: *1- 888-778-0033*
Email: *info@miltonandhugo.com*

Ordering Information:
Quantity sales. Special discounts are granted to corporations, associations, and other organizations. For more information on these discounts, please reach out to the publisher using the contact information provided above.

ISBN-13: 979-8-89285-859-5 [Paperback Edition]
979-8-89285-858-8 [Digital Edition]

Rev. date: 05/11/2026

CHAPTER ONE

The Boys Band Concert

One day, Megan, Sierra, Sasha, and Brandi went to Wal-Mart to do some shopping. While shopping, they ran into Bob Patrick of Kissin 92.5 radio station. He told them that they could register for tickets to see The Boys Band in concert. Sasha asked, "Where at?"

Bob said, "In Las Vegas."

They signed up for the tickets. A week later Megan and Brandi were sitting and watching The Boys Band on a video tape when the phone rang. It was Bob Patrick. He said they won the tickets to see The Boys Band in Las Vegas and they leave in two days on a plane. They were so happy. Two days later, they were riding in a taxi to Joplin Airport to board a plane for Las Vegas to see The Boys Band in concert.

Brandi and Megan were singing songs from TBB like "Around the World for You, "It's the Meaning of

You, and "It's The Boys Band." Sierra was telling her mom, Sasha, that she couldn't believe they get to miss school to see TBB in concert. She was all excited that she kept asking when it was. Brandi said, "Sunday, October 17th, 1999."

Brandi was just so crazy for TBB — well mostly for Jeremy Eugene. She knew everything there was to know about him. She even tells herself that she will marry him. She considered herself the second biggest fan, because his sister was his biggest fan. They were walking on the plane and Megan got nervous that she almost threw up. Brandi told her that everything would be alright and she was on her way to see the best band ever, besides, God was flying with them. They were seated and soon were up in the air.

Two hours later, they were at Las Vegas airport getting off the plane and a limo was waiting to take them to the hotel. They got in and flipped out at all the cool stuff. A cellphone, a fridge, a TV, a CD player, and a DVD player. Sasha called her boyfriend Eric and was telling him all about the cool stuff in the limo. Megan was listening to TBB on the CD player and Sierra was watching TV. Brandi raided the fridge for wine and beer. By the time they reached the hotel, Brandi was so drunk that Sasha and the bell boy had to carry her to her room. They were so amazed at the room that they almost passed out at the sight. Brandi, of course, has already passed out.

The room was so gorgeous. It had two bedrooms with flower curtains and silk bedding. A big tub that looked like a pool, and a walk-in shower that could fit 20 people. Megan told herself that only The Boys Band would do this for their fans. They went to bed early because tomorrow night is the concert. Megan and Brandi got up early, around eight in the morning, and took a shower. They got dressed and left Sasha and Sierra saying they were going shopping for the concert tonight. They called the front desk to ask for the limo driver, Earl, to pick them up. They went everywhere that morning. They ended up with a lot of things, such as shoes, clothes, and jewelry for the concert tonight. Megan bought bell bottoms and a black top that hangs off the shoulders that went with her platform shoes. Brandi got a yellow tank top that said 'Phantom of the Opera' in black. She also got black wide leg jeans and a pair of black platform sandals. She had her blonde hair done in curls.

As they were heading up stairs to their room and busy talking, they ran into Jeremy Eugene and J Baby of The Boys Band. They dropped the stuff they were holding. Brandi looked down to see Jeremy Eugene squatting down to pick up her stuff. He spoke to her and asked her if she was alright. Brandi shook her head to say "yes". Jeremy Eugene looked down at Brandi's shirt that said "Phantom of the Opera." Jeremy Eugene asked her if she loved it. She responded with a yes. He said he loved it, too. Baby J laughed and said, "Here he goes again."

Megan asked what he meant by that. Baby J told her that Jeremy Eugene is a big flirt. Baby J looked at Megan and asked for her name. She told him and they shook hands. Travis Van came running down the hall. He was yelling at Jeremy Eugene and Baby J to hurry up. Jeremy Eugene handed Brandi back her stuff. Brandi and Megan left saying they couldn't believe they ran into Jeremy Eugene and Baby J of TBB. Jeremy Eugene watched Brandi walk away until she and Megan were in their room. He turned around and yelled, "I can't believe I forgot to ask her name."

Brandi and Megan told Sasha and Sierra all about bumping into Jeremy Eugene and Baby J from The Boys Band. The girls didn't believe them, but that was alright. Brandi and Megan knew the truth. They all started getting ready for the concert. When it was time to go, they all piled into the limo. As they arrived, they all jumped out. There were tons of girls waiting outside to go in. Brandi, Megan, Sierra, and Sasha was escorted in the theater. They sat down in the fourth row. All the rest of the people came in chanting, "We want TBB!" Suddenly a voice came on, which sounded like Joe, saying "Kill the lights!" It went dark.

A flash of lights went off and the guys came down over the heads of the audience. Everyone was screaming. Jeremy Eugene looked down and saw a yellow tank top with the words that said Phantom of the Opera. Brandi looked up and saw Jeremy Eugene right over her. He was wearing black pants and a white long sleeve shirt. He pointed to Brandi and mouthed, "It's you."

They started singing and flying to the stage. Brandi started crying because Jeremy Eugene remembered her. They opened with their popular song and then some old ones. Then they sang solo songs. Baby J came out to sing his song "Only You." Baby J was wearing a black suit. Megan started to scream, "I Love You!" Baby J noticed Megan and got off the stage. He was holding her hand and singing to her. He then whispered in her ear, "Hey nice to see you."

He returned back to the stage. After Baby J got off the stage, he went to Zack and told him to go to the girl in the fourth row with the blonde hair, wearing a blue shirt when he does his solo to give her a white rose.

Zack came out in black jeans and no shirt. He had dozen white roses in his hand. He started singing his song "My Heart is Yours." He was throwing out his white roses. When he got to the last one, he spotted the girl Baby J was talking about. He walked off the stage and handed the last white rose to Sierra with a kiss on the hand. Zack then went back on stage to finish his solo. Sierra told Megan she liked Zack more than ever.

Jeremy came out in a brown jacket with no shirt and black jeans. He bowed and said he would like to dedicate this song to the most beautiful girl he has ever seen and pointed to Brandi in the crowd. He started to sing his solo song called, "Inside You." When his song was over, he left the stage so Joe could do his solo. Joe sang his song, "I Can't Believe What She Said." All of them came back to the stage to finish the show. They sang the song, "This Is Us". A bunch of different colored lights flashed and then it went black. The concert is officially over.

The girls went back to the hotel room to pack. The next morning, they got ready to go to the airport to go back home. Brandi and Megan hurried up, so they could wait in the hallway to see if Jeremy and Baby J would come out. Sasha and Sierra finished before, so they went down to the lobby to wait for the limo. The guys finally got to the hotel after all the after-parties. Jeremy went to the front desk to see if he could find out about the blonde girl he ran into yesterday. He couldn't get information on her as the policy of the hotel is that they don't share guest information. He was upset as he was walking to the elevators. He thought he would never see her again. As he was walking back to his room, he then remembered they walked into a room. He ran down to see the room number and went back to his room to call the front desk. Some woman answered. He told her who he was and that he needed help with something. The woman was all giddy and said she could help him with whatever he wanted. Jeremy asked who was in Room 360. She said it was under a radio station called Kissin 92.5. Jeremy thanked her and hung up.

Meanwhile, Brandi, Sasha, Megan, and Sierra were on a plane back to Joplin, Missouri. Brandi couldn't wait to tell everyone. She was also sad because she would never see Jeremy again. The Boys Band was on a bus to go to the next concert. Jeremy Eugene was on the phone with Kissin 92.5 radio station asking who won the tickets to his concert in Las Vegas. In the meantime, Brandi and the girls was off the plane in Joplin, Missouri. They were waiting for Eric, Sasha's boyfriend, to pick them up. They all got back to Sasha's house and went to bed.

The next day, Brandi went back home. She told her mom all about the concert and meeting Jeremy Eugene from The Boys Band. Her mom said that was so awesome. She then told Brandi there was a surprise in her bedroom. Jesse, Brandi's brother, walked in. Brandi got really excited. She had not seen him for six months because he was in California. He told her all about the beach and she told him all about Las Vegas.

A month later, Jeremy and the band was in Kansas City, Missouri, when he got a call from Kissin 92.5 radio station. They told him the name of the person who won the Las Vegas tickets — it was Brandi Dunn. Jeremy asked Baby J if he wanted to take a two hour trip to Joplin to find the beautiful blonde that was named Brandi Dunn. He said, "Sure". He wanted to see Megan anyways.

In the meantime, at Brandi's house there was a party that started for her brother's birthday. Brandi's ex showed up with his best friend and his brother. Tobias walked up to Brandi and told her that her yellow tank top was very sexy. Brandi said thank you and told him she bought it in Las Vegas. Tobias said, "That's right. You went to see the fag boys in concert."

Brandi said, "Well, Jeremy Eugene didn't seem gay when I met him in the hotel." She then turned around and walked off.

Jeremy and Baby J was at the radio station in Joplin. Bob Patrick told them that the address was 2903 West 3rd. Bob printed out MapQuest for them to find the place. They found the address and knocked on the door. Sasha answered the door and was shocked to find Jeremy Eugene and Baby J. Jeremy asked if Brandi was there. Just then, Megan walked into the room. Baby J got excited and waved to Megan and Megan smiled. Jeremy asked her where Brandi was. She told him Brandi was at her house and she could take them there. They got into a rental car and arrived at Brandi's. Jeremy's heart was pounding when he saw Brandi sitting on the porch. Megan gave a disgusted moan. Baby J asked what was wrong. Megan told him that the guy standing beside her was Brandi's ex and she didn't like him for hurting Brandi. Jeremy said he would take care of him.

Brandi noticed a red jeep pulling up. She stood up when she saw Jeremy driving. Jeremy came to a stop and jumped out yelling, "Hello, my beautiful girlfriend!" Brandi played along. She ran out to him and gave him a very long passionate kiss. When they pulled away, Megan said, "Wow! That was a true love's kiss." Brandi smiled and turned to Tobias who had a mad look on his face.

Jeremy said, "I had to see my Brandi Eugene." Brandi went wide eyed.

"You said Brandi Eugene."

Jeremy said, "Yes. I know we are fated for each other. We are getting married. Do you want to get married?"

Brandi's dad yelled, "Marry him! I like him."

Everybody started to laugh except for Tobias. Brandi shook her head to say yes. Tobias walked off the porch to get in his friend's car. Tobias, his friend, and his brother drove off. Brandi got ahold of their old family pastor. She told him she wanted to get married as soon as possible.

They then drove back to Kansas City for the concert. At the end of the concert, Jeremy told the audience that he had a surprise. Brandi walked out with the pastor. He performed the ceremony on stage and pronounced them husband and wife. The crowd went wild. Jeremy and Brandi was so happy.

CHAPTER TWO

Jeremy Eugene and Brandi

It had been five years since Jeremy and Brandi got married. In those five years, Jeremy and Brandi got their own house down the street from Joe and his girlfriend, Leann, in Florida. Sasha lived in Florida for a couple of years. She moved back to Missouri and met someone nice, rich, and very handsome. He owned a ranch with horses, cows, and lots of dogs. Sierra was happy to be there. She loved the ranch boy. Every day she would go out to talk to him. Sierra thought to herself that he was the spitting image of Zack. As for Megan, she lived with Jeremy and Brandi. She just couldn't leave Baby J. Baby J was seeing other girls.

Brandi got a job as a laundry attendant. She got her dream car. A 1964 ½ Ford Mustang convertible. It is white with a black interior.

Brandi found that she was pregnant with twins. A boy and a girl. Jeremy took nine months off from touring so he could be with Brandi. Brandi drove Jeremy crazy during that time. Her cravings were pickles and burritos 24-7. The next months were hard on them. The lovemaking was totally gone. Then one night, as Megan was playing the PlayStation, Brandi went into labor. Megan called Cheryl, Jeremy's mom, to tell her that Brandi went into labor. Cheryl picked up Brandi to take her to the hospital.

Jeremy showed up just before Brandi delivered the twins. The first baby came out. It was a boy. Two hours later, the second baby came out. It was a girl. Jeremy and Brandi named the boy Wyatt Wayne. They named the girl Draven Vaughn. Brandi was in the hospital for three days. When she got out of the hospital, Jeremy and Megan were there to pick her up. When they got home, Joe, Leann, Zack, Baby J, and Travis were there. Later, Cheryl showed up. Everyone was in awe of the twins. They said Draven looked like a little girl version of Jeremy, and Wyatt looked like a little boy version of Brandi. Brandi was so tired that she went to bed. Megan went with her. She was so mad at Baby J.

The next day, Brandi woke up early before anybody else. She walked down the hall to the nursery. She found Jeremy sleeping in the rocking chair next to the cribs. Brandi covered him with a blanket and kissed him on the forehead. She looked at her babies. She thought to herself that it had been a year since she talked to her family back home. She had to get in touch with them since she had her babies. Jeremy woke up to see Brandi looking at the twins. He sensed that Brandi was sad. He knew it because she missed her family. He got up to order plane tickets to go back to Missouri. Later that night, they were on a plane back to Missouri with the twins. Brandi was so happy to surprise her family.

Baby J texted Megan and told her that he would miss her.

When they landed at the airport in Joplin, Jeremy rented a car for them all to get to the hotel. They freshened up and then drove to Brandi's parents in Galena, Kansas. When they pulled up, they saw Brandi's uncle, Carey, outside. Brandi got out first and said hello. Her uncle Carey said, "Hello. It's been a long time." Brandi grabbed Wyatt and his diaper bag. She walked up to her uncle and gave him a hug. She then walked into her parents' house. Jeremy grabbed Draven and her diaper bag. He helped Megan out of the backseat. They walked into the house.

Her mom was sitting on a purple flowered couch next to the window. Her dad was sitting in an old tan recliner by the fireplace. Her brother was standing in the doorway from the living room to the kitchen. Tobias, her ex, was sitting on the couch next to her mom and the doorway. Her mom jumped up and yelled, "Oh my god!" She was running to Brandi to hug her when she noticed a baby in her arms. She stopped dead in her tracks. She asked whose baby boy it was. Brandi said, "This is your grandson, Wyatt Wayne Eugene. His middle name is after Dad." Her mom got all excited. Just then, Jeremy said, "But wait, there is more." Tina turned to Jeremy to see a baby girl. Tina went wide-eyed and said, "Twins?" Jeremy said, "Yes. This is Draven Vaughn. She is named after your side of the family." Brandi's mom grabbed Draven out of Jeremy's arms. Fred, Brandi's dad, grabbed Wyatt from her arms.

Megan went to sit by Tobias and Carey since he came in from outside. Tobias asked Megan how Florida was. She told him it was great. The best place ever. Brandi sat down on the arm of the couch next to the window. Jeremy sat on the floor in front of the coffee table. Brandi asked how Tobias was. He replied, "Great. Partying all the time and getting it while I can." Brandi laughed and rolled her eyes.

Just then Brandi's aunt Angie pulled up. She came inside and noticed Brandi, sitting on the arm of the couch next to her uncle Carey. Angie walked over to hug her niece. She then turned around and saw two newborn babies. She looked at Brandi and asked if they were hers. Brandi nodded yes. Carey got up so Angie could sit down and hold the twins. Angie asked for their names. Brandi said, "The boy is Wyatt Wayne, and the girl is Draven Vaughn." Jeremy asked Tina if Sasha still lived on the ranch. Tina nodded yes. Jeremy looked at Megan and asked if she wanted to go see her mom and sister, Sierra. Megan jumped up and said, "Hell yes!" Jeremy kissed Brandi and walked out the door.

Tina asked Brandi when the twins were born. She said four days ago. Tina's and Angie's mouths fell open. They both said at the same time, "And you flew here?" Brandi shook her head yes. Angie asked for her cravings. Brandi had told her about burritos and pickles. Tobias said, "Yuck." Brandi told him he should try and be pregnant.

Meanwhile, Jeremy and Megan arrived at the ranch. They saw Sierra riding a horse. Megan got out and shouted at Sierra. Sierra got off her horse and ran to Megan. They hugged as Sasha came out of the house. All three women hugged as Jeremy stared on. Sasha pulled back and asked where Brandi was at. Jeremy told her that she was at her parents' house.

Meanwhile, Angie, Tina, Brandi, and Tobias went to see a love story with Brad Pitt. Angie sat by Tina, Brandi sat by her mom, and Tobias sat next to Brandi. They sat in the middle of the fourth row. Brandi told everyone that she was friends with two of the co-stars. Joe and Leann. Tobias didn't believe her. Brandi pulled out her cellphone. She showed pictures of Joe and Leann. She said, "Wait until the movie starts and see if you recognize them."

Angie said she couldn't believe she was married to someone famous. Tobias told her to shut up. After the movie, Tobias said he couldn't believe Brandi was right about knowing Joe and Leann.

They dropped Tina off at home so she could spend time with her grandbabies. Then Angie, Brandi, and Tobias went to her house and met up with Tobias's brother, Adam. They all started playing poker. Brandi was winning while Tobias was getting drunk. He was getting all handsy with Brandi. She kept trying to push him away. She kept telling him that she was married. He told her that they were meant to be. Brandi told him that it was a teenage affair. Just then, there was a knock on the door.

Jeremy walked in to see Tobias was trying to put his hands down Brandi's shirt. Jeremy ran over to him and grabbed his hand. He twisted it back and clenched his teeth together saying, "Take your fucking hands off my wife." Tobias said through clenched teeth, "She was mine and will always be mine." Jeremy said, "You messed that up long ago." He dragged Tobias to the door and threw him down the steps of the porch. Brandi and Jeremy told Angie sorry and left. They drove in silence back to Brandi's parents' house. They picked up the kids and drove to the hotel. They put the babies in the crib. Jeremy turned to look at Brandi to say sorry. Brandi had so much lust and desire in her eyes. Jeremy grabbed her and pushed her up against the wall. He kissed her passionately. He whispered in her ear, "You are my soulmate. You are my breath in the morning and my last sigh at night. I knew that the first time I saw you in the hallway at a hotel in Las Vegas. It'll always be this way until death do us part and after." They lay down in bed and cuddled all night.

The next morning, Brandi got a call from her brother, Jesse. He said there was trouble at their mom and dad's house and to bring Jeremy. They got the babies ready. They dropped the twins to Megan at Sasha's; they told her there was trouble at Tina's. When they arrived, they saw Tobias, Adam, and two other guys drunk off their asses. Brandi's dad Fred was outside, trying to fight them alone. Brandi jumped out of the car. She took a swing at one of the guys with Tobias. The guy went flying back to the ground. He staggered up and tried to take a swing at Brandi. That was a big no.

Jeremy, Tobias, Adam, and Fred went after him. They each punched the guy. The guy got up and left with the other guy. Tobias looked at Jeremy. He said, "I'm sorry. I just thought Brandi was too good for me let alone someone else famous or not. I can now see real true love in you guys." Tobias shook Jeremy's hand and walked over to hug Brandi for their last goodbye.

Jesse got in the car with Tobias and Adam to take them home. Brandi and Jeremy were driving to go pick up the twins when the guy that got beaten up drove up behind them. He slammed right into them. He then drove up next to them and ran right into them on the driver's side door. He hit so hard and flipped the car over onto its side. Jeremy was on the passenger side. Brandi looked up to see drunk guy drive off. She looked at Jeremy to see he was out cold. She tried to wake him up, but he didn't respond. Brandi reached into her pocket and pulled out her cellphone. She called 911 and gave her location and what happened.

The ambulance showed up; they took them to the hospital. When Brandi was done getting checked out, she went to find out about her husband Jeremy. She found a nurse and asked about him. She told Brandi that he was in room 420. Brandi walked down to Jeremy's room. The doctor was in there. The doctor turned around to see Brandi. He asked her if he could help her. Brandi told him that Jeremy was her husband. The doctor said that Jeremy was in a coma. Brandi started to cry. She fell to her knees. The doctor ran to Brandi. He helped her up and sat her on a chair in the room. He told her that Jeremy can come out of this. He told her to talk with him and to get all his loved ones too, because he could hear them. The doctor left the room. Brandi called everyone she could think of. She then grabbed Jeremy's hand. She was crying so bad. She tried to speak but couldn't.

A few hours later, all of Brandi's family showed up to help support Brandi during this time. A few hours later, all the guys from The Boys Band showed up, along with Jeremy's mom, Cheryl. Brandi left them in the room to sit with Jeremy. Brandi sat in the waiting room when Jeremy's ex, Amanda, walked in. She slapped Brandi in the face and said through clenched teeth. "You gold-digging whore. You took my man, and now he will die because of you." Amanda spat in Brandi's face. She grabbed Brandi by the hair to drag her to the ground. Just then, Baby J walked in and grabbed Amanda by the arm. He yelled, "Get off Brandi! She just had babies." Amanda looked surprised and disgusted at the same time. She said, "Oh, you think having his babies has you locked in for life? Nice try. I'm going to get him back. You and your little demons will be out on your asses." Baby J called for security to throw Amanda out. Brandi thanked Baby J. Baby J said no problem and told Brandi to call him by his real name, Josh. Brandi laughed and said, "Okay."

Josh asked Brandi where Megan was at. Brandi said at Sasha's, taking care of the twins. Josh told her he had to make things right with Megan and asked Brandi if he could win her heart back. Brandi told him that it has very high possibility. A month had passed and Jeremy was still in a coma.

One day, Brandi was in the room, telling Jeremy about Wyatt and Draven when Amanda showed up. She grabbed Brandi by the neck and started choking her. Brandi tried to scream, but to no avail. When she thought she was going to die, she prayed to God to forgive Amanda for what she was doing and to wake Jeremy from his coma to take car of their babies. Brandi's eyes started roll back into her head, but then there was a release. Brandi opened her eyes to see

Jeremy out of bed and had Amanda on the floor, saying, "Leave my true love alone. I don't, nor have I ever or will ever, love you, Amanda."

A month later, Brandi, Jeremy, and the twins were on a plane back home. Cheryl was there to pick them up and to take them home. As they arrived home, Cheryl said she was taking the twins home so Jeremy and Brandi could be alone after all of this. They went upstairs to their room. Jeremy slammed the door and pushed Brandi up against the wall. He whispered in her ear, "All I thought about was taking you, like a big daddy should, and make you cum like a good girl should and then have you beg me for more." Brandi started to breathe heavily. She closed her eyes as Jeremy put little kisses on her neck, and then he started to nibble on her ear. Just like that Jeremy went to his knees and was between her legs. She begged for him for more. Jeremy was very pleased to do it again and again all night.

CHAPTER THREE

The Marriage

A month later, everyone was setting up for Joe and Leann's wedding. Megan was to be the maid of honor; Brandi and Sierra were to be the bridesmaids. One of Leann's nieces was the flower girl. Josh was the best man, Jeremy and Zack were the groomsmen, and Travis was the ring boy, to make the ceremony funny. Joe was looking out over the crowd. He noticed Megan and Josh were all lovey-dovey. He thought to himself that they would be next to marry. He saw Jeremy and Brandi. He thought to himself that he was happy his friend made it through his horrible ordeal. He hoped his marriage to Leann would be as true as Jeremy and Brandi's. Just then, Zack came up to Joe and asked him if he was ready to marry the love of his life. Joe nodded his head. As Zack walked away, he noticed Sierra talking on her cellphone to her boyfriend Clint. He wondered when she got so beautiful. Everyone took their place. Joe was so nervous. The music began, and out walked Brandi and Jeremy, then Sierra and Zack, then Megan and Josh. Travis walked out dancing with Leann's niece. Everyone laughed. The music changed to "Here Comes the Bride." Everyone shut up and looked at Leann. She was so beautiful. After the "I dos," everyone went to the reception. The Boys Band sang a couple of songs before the Backstreet Boys performed for the rest of the night. Love was in the air.

CHAPTER FOUR

Josh and Megan

It had been two years since Joe and Leann got married. They moved to Kentucky on a farm to raise their little boy, James. Zack met a girl named Sharon. They have been dating for a year now. Travis quit being a player and started dating actress Mandy Maye. Jeremy and Brandi have been going strong. They still act like they were on their honeymoon. Sierra broke up with Clint, the ranch boy. She began dating singer Justin Curl. She met him through Brandi and Jeremy. Josh and Megan have worked things out and were getting married.

Brandi was sitting on the couch when Megan walked in. They was discussing the plans with Brandi, Leann, and Mandy. Sierra was to be the maid of honor. Josh's older brother was the best man. Jeremy, Joe, and Travis were the groomsmen. They were going to have a December wedding in Orlando, Florida. They had their own bachelor and bachelorette parties. Megan's party had singers like Kid Rock, Korn, Snoop Dog, and Eminem there. Josh had his at Planet Hollywood.

The next day, Megan and the girls woke up early to get ready. The guys were a little too hungover to get up early. Megan was so nervous. She was bridezilla. Sasha came in and helped calm her down.

Jeremy woke up at 10:00 a.m. He frantically got up to get everyone awake, since the wedding was to start at 1:00 p.m. The guys all got up one by one to take showers. Jeremy and Joe decorated the limo when they got to the church.

Brandi looked around the church to see how beautiful it was. There were fake snow and snowflakes hanging from the ceiling. White candles on silver stands were everywhere. She then headed to the reception area. The tables were white with silk back wooden chairs. Each table had clear vases with white roses inside. She finally reached Megan in the dressing room.

It was now 12:50 p.m. Everyone was taking their place. Josh was at the altar. Sierra and Josh's brother walked out, then it was Brandi and Jeremy, then it was Joe and Leann, then it was Travis and Mandy, and then it was the flower girl and the ring boy. The music started playing, and it was "Winter Wonderland." Out came Megan and her dad, Bill. Megan had a white dress on. It had snowflakes as the patterns. She has a silver crown on her head. Josh was crying when she arrived at the altar. They said their "I dos."

Everyone went to the reception room. Josh and Megan danced to their wedding song, "It's Your Love." They cut the cake later. The night had ended, and they left for their honeymoon in Hawaii.

CHAPTER FIVE

Zack's Affair

It had been a year since Josh and Megan got married. They moved to a farm in Lexington, Kentucky. They've been trying to have a baby. Joe and Leann lived down the road and were doing great with their son. Jeremy and Brandi were going good with the twins. Travis was back to dating everyone in sight. Everyone was wondering if he would grow up.

The band was doing great. They just finished their fifth album. They would start touring in a couple of months. Everyone was happy, but Zack. He wanted to settle down and get married. His girlfriend ended up moving to England.

One day, Zack was at Jeremy's house, visiting, when Sierra walked in to see Brandi. Zack got an instant feeling of passion over him after seeing her. She looked so amazing with her long blond hair falling past her sweet round ass. He looked at her emerald-green eyes just glowing. Her smile was wide and so white. Zack pulled his eyes and thoughts away from Sierra.

Brandi came down the stairs to see Sierra. Sierra asked Brandi if she wanted to go shopping. Brandi shook her head yes. Zack visited for a couple more hours and decided to go home and take a nap.

Two hours had passed, and there was a knock on the door. Zack got up to answer it. It was Sierra, crying. Zack let her in and asked what was wrong. Sierra said it was Travis. She told him that they were seeing each other in private. She found him with another girl. Zack wrapped his arms around Sierra. He held her until she calmed down. Sierra finally calmed down and felt something poking her into her belly. She looked down to see Zack was hard. She then looked up at Zack. Zack had a half grin and said he was sorry. He doesn't know why he had these feelings all of a sudden. Sierra reached up and pulled his head so they could kiss. They were kissing passionately, then Zack picked her up and carried her to the bedroom. The had the most amazing sex ever.

In the morning, Sierra awoke and got dressed. She rushed to Brandi's to tell her what happened. When she got there, she saw Sharon was there. Sharon hugged her and told her she was happy to see her. She said she was in town to surprise Zack.

Sierra asked if she could speak to Brandi alone and grabbed her by the arm. She took her upstairs to Brandi's bedroom. Sierra told Brandi everything that happened with Zack. Sierra asked what she should do now that Sharon was back. Brandi said it was up to Zack who he wanted to be with.

Sharon showed up at Zack's. She walked in and heard Zack say, "Why, did you leave without saying bye?" Zack turned to see it was Sharon and not Sierra. Sharon gave him a weird look. She said, "I did say goodbye." Zack said, "Never mind. What are you doing here?" Sharon told him that she was ready to settle down now. Zack looked long at her. He finally said that he slept with Sierra. Sharon's mouth dropped. Zack said he had feelings for Sierra. He couldn't be with Sharon until he figured out what his heart really wanted. Sharon walked up to him and kissed his cheek. She told him sorry for not wanting marriage when he was ready. She told him that she was going back to England until he decided what he wanted.

CHAPTER SIX

Zack's Life

It has been three months since Zack's affair. The band went on a tour of Europe. They were home for a month before they toured the US. Zack hasn't been with Sierra or Sharon. He thought it was best to be by himself for the tour. The band had a press conference to do. At the press conference, a reporter asked how he felt that his ex, Sharon, was pregnant with their baby. He said he had no reply. After the conference, he called Sharon to see if it was true. Sharon said it was true. Zack set up a time to meet with her. They met, and Zack wanted to do a DNA test. Sharon agreed to it. A week later, they were at the doctor's office. They injected a needle into Sharon to get blood from the baby inside her. Two days later, Zack got a call saying the DNA didn't match his. Zack called Sharon to tell her the baby wasn't his. She said it was right. She slept with someone else but used it as an excuse to get him back. Zack told her that she was evil and to stay out of his life for good. He called Sierra up. He told her what happened, and he was sorry it took so long to let her know that it was her he chose. Sierra asked if they could meet up. Zack told her to come over. Sierra showed up, and they made love all night long. In the morning, Zack asked Sierra to marry him. Sierra said she had waited so long for that question. She shook her head yes.

CHAPTER SEVEN

This Too Shall Pass

It has been a year since Sierra and Zack got engaged. They've been planning a big wedding. They lived on the southern coast of Florida. Joe and Leann were doing good. Leann was directing movies. She recently directed a movie called We've Got It Going On. When Joe and the Guys were not touring, Joe did a revival in Kentucky. Jeremy and Brandi were truly happy. The twins, Wyatt and Draven, were now five. They would start school in the fall. Jeremy's mom, Cheryl, was very sick and stayed home a lot. Josh and Megan were not doing well now. Megan wasn't able to have kids. Josh was always going to do something. Sasha, Megan's mom, just passed away. She was murdered by her boyfriend's mistress. The mistress got life in prison.

Travis married some strange woman in Las Vegas. One day, Josh walked in and gave Megan the divorce papers. Megan cried as she signed the papers. Megan left to see Leann. Leann had called Brandi and told her what happened. Brandi told her to call Sierra so they could fly out there to see Megan. Brandi and Sierra landed in Kentucky a couple of hours later. Brandi rented an Airbnb so they could stay together with Megan. Leann brought Megan over, and all four binge-watched rom-coms and ate their fill of popcorn, ice cream, and chips. They all passed out on the floor around 3:00 a.m. After a week of being in the Airbnb, they emerged like vampires in the sunlight. Leann hugged everyone goodbye and went to get started packing Megan's stuff. Megan decided to leave and stay with Brandi and Jeremy. Sierra had to go back to plan her wedding.

When they all got back home, Brandi found out that Cheryl was in the hospital. She wasn't doing good. The doctors ran every test. It was a matter of weeks left. Brandi called everyone to tell them. Almost two weeks went by, and everyone had gathered to say their goodbyes to Cheryl.

Josh brought a new woman with him named Elizabeth. She had a ring on. Brandi threw a fit and said that Megan didn't need to see this, and Cheryl didn't even know this woman and told Josh to get rid of her. Everyone agreed with Brandi and told Josh to leave. The doctor came out and said Cheryl had passed. Jeremy grabbed Brandi and held her so tight and was crying uncontrollably. The funeral was a week later. The pastor said, "This too shall pass." Everyone thought how true this statement was.

CHAPTER EIGHT

Death of a The Boys Band Member

It has been five years since Cheryl Eugene passed away and five years since Josh and Megan divorced. In those five years, a lot has happened. Josh's new bride, Kristen, was a backup dancer for Cher. Big whoopie. They went to Las Vegas to get married. No one was with them. Sierra and Zack had a baby boy. They never come around unless it's for the band. Joe and Leann were always happy together. Jeremy and Brandi have moved from Florida. There were too many memories of Cheryl there. They moved to New Orleans. Brandi didn't like it too well. Britney Spears lived down the road. She was always coming over to talk to Jeremy. The twins were now ten. Travis was still acting wild and couldn't settle down. Megan has been dating around. She has finally found out that she couldn't carry kids. She adopted a girl named Cara Jennette.

You think from the way things were going that life for all these people was peachy, but you're wrong. Life for certain people was about to take a turn for the worse.

Joe was in the living room while Leann was in bed asleep. Joe was in pain and could barely breathe. He dialed 911 on his phone.

Meanwhile, Jeremy was in the pool while Britney showed up and talked to him. She jumped into the pool and grabbed Jeremy by the shoulders and kissed him. Brandi came out of the sliding doors. She yelled, "How could you, Jeremy!" Jeremy pulled away to see Brandi run to the house.

Meanwhile, Megan was at the hospital with the baby. She was having breathing problems. The doctor said she had a heart defect. Meanwhile, Josh and Kristen were fighting. Kristen wanted to go to Europe for the Cher tour; Josh wanted her to stay. Just then, the phone rang. It was Leann telling him that Joe was in the hospital with a heart attack.

Jeremy got out of the pool. He ran after Brandi. Brandi was packing her clothes and calling the airport to get tickets to Missouri. Jeremy came in and told her no.

Meanwhile, Megan heard a nurse say there was a flat line in room 203. Megan ran to her daughter's room, only to be pushed out.

Josh arrived at the hospital. He was going to call everyone about Joe when he saw Leann coming out crying. He ran to her, and she told him Joe had passed away. They held each other.

Meanwhile, Megan got the news that her daughter had passed away. She bawled her eyes out and called Sierra.

Jeremy wrapped his arms around Brandi and told her what happened. He said he wanted Brandi for life, and he would ban Britney from coming over. Britney walked in and Brandi told her how dare she come into her house, let alone her room. Jeremy told Britney to leave and never come back, or the cops will be called. Just then, everyone got the call about Joe's death.

CHAPTER NINE

The Pack

Funeral time. Everyone arrived. The preacher talked and prayed. Leann and Josh talked and sang. Everyone then left.

It had been a year since Joe's death. Leann and Josh started seeing each other. Josh divorced Kristen.

Megan lived in Australia. She met a man who was a widower and has a son named Merlin Jack. Sierra and Zack were still married and living in Florida. Sierra was pregnant with twin girls.

Brandi and Jeremy lived in Missouri still and loved it.

Josh and Leann were in the middle of having sex. Josh said he couldn't handle living in Joe's house. "Too many memories," and he got off Leann. He got dressed and walked out the door.

Sierra and Zack were lying in bed when the twins kicked. Zack started yelling that he felt them.

Leann kept trying to call Josh, but it went straight to voicemail.

Megan was outside with her stepson. A big snake came upon them. It had bitten her while she was trying to protect her stepson.

Leann decided to go to the church that Joe and Josh used to go to. Josh was at the altar. He heard her coming and told her that he knew she would show up and told her she could watch what he was about to do. He grabbed a rope to hang himself. Leann yelled no at him. She grabbed her cellphone out of her purse to call 911. They came in time to stop him. They put him in jail for the night. A woman came to bring Josh food. When she came back to grab the dishes, she forgot to grab the plastic knife. Josh jammed his wrist with a plastic knife. By the time the woman noticed what she did, Josh had bled out and died. Leann was called and began crying.

Megan was sent to the hospital. She got the antidote just in time.

Everyone got a call from Leann, saying Josh killed himself while in police custody.

A week later, everyone met at Leann's for Josh's funeral. It was a very sad time. After the funeral, Jeremy gathered everyone around. He started to tell them that once a year, everyone needed to get together in Orlando and spend a week there for Joe's and Josh's memories and to check in on everyone's emotional needs. Everyone agreed to do that.

CHAPTER TEN

Life Is Important

It had been ten years since Josh's death. In those years a lot has happened. Jeremy and Brandi lived in Scotland and have grandkids. Wyatt got married when he turned eighteen. His wife was called Angel; they just had a baby boy named Bradford. Draven was an actress and lived in Hollywood. Wyatt lived in Florida.

Zack and Sierra were in Florida with the twins. They were ten, and they were named Angela and Angie. Zack had his own band now. Sierra was part of the band, and it was called Zack and His Angels. It's a gospel band. The band was big in the South.

Megan lived in New York with her new boyfriend of two years. He was up-and-coming Broadway star named Ryan Zeek.

Leann took Josh's death really hard. She got into drugs. She became an adult film actress. One day she was so high that she couldn't perform. The director was so mad that he killed her with a wrench. Her son lived on a ranch in South Dakota. He was adopted long ago.

Brandi was standing in the kitchen and washing the dishes. Jeremy walked up behind her. Brandi could sense he was there. She laughed, and Jeremy said she always knew when he showed up. They hugged and ended up making love on the kitchen table.

Sierra was sitting in the living room, doing Angie's hair. She has head lice. Sierra got up and found blood and thought it was weird because she just got off her period last week. She went to see her doctor. He ran some tests and told her that she was bleeding from her ovaries. He told her to go to Los Angles because they were better equipped for her. They left the next day to go to Los Angles. When they arrived, Sierra went straight to the doctor. He looked her over. He said she needed surgery to take everything, or she would die. They scheduled the surgery in two days.

In that time, everyone found out about it and flew in to be there for Zack and Sierra. Sierra couldn't believe that Brandi and Jeremy came in from Scotland. Brandi told her that was what families do. Everyone caught up on life when Sierra went into surgery. Everyone was happy that Brandi and Jeremy were grandparents.

A couple of hours later, Sierra was out of surgery. Everyone went in to see her. Two days later, she was back home with Zack and the girls. She thought to herself that life was so important.

CHAPTER ELEVEN

Megan's third Wedding

It has been a year since Ryan Zeek proposed to Megan. In that year, not much has happened. Everyone was planning the wedding for Megan and Ryan. It was six in the morning when Brandi and Sierra knocked on Megan's door. Megan opened it, and the girls rushed in, saying it was the wedding day. Ryan woke up to look at the clock. It was 10:00 a.m. He got up to find all the guys at the table eating cereal. He asked them why they didn't wake him. Jeremy told him that he could sleep in. All they had to do was get dressed and head to the church. The girls would probably be late. Ryan asked how he knew that. Jeremy told him that they had all been to six weddings already.

Megan got her hair done in a bun with roses around it. Off-white nails with blue dots, and her dress was off-white. It was long and sparkly and tight on her small figure. The flowers she held were blue roses.

It was time to walk down the aisle. Brandi said she looked like an angel. Sierra was Megan's matron of honor. She had a long blue dress and held one white rose. Brandi was the bridesmaid. She had a long white dress and was holding a single blue rose. Zack was standing at the altar with Jeremy as his best man.

The organ started to play the "Wedding March." In walked Sierra and Brandi. Zack and Jeremy looked at their wives and fell in love again. Then in walked Megan. Everyone stood up and was in awe of her beauty. Megan reached Ryan's side. The pastor said the wedding vows. When he got to the part, "Does anyone object…," the doors opened, and Ryan's ex came in and said, "I object." She said she was carrying his baby. Megan said it was a lie. They had been together for three years. Ryan looked at her and said he cheated. Megan slapped him and ran out of the church. Brandi slapped Ryan and ran out looking for Megan. She caught up with her. Megan said she wanted to go back home to Missouri.

A week later, Megan was at her dad's house. She was dreaming about Josh. He had come back for her, and when she was about to touch him, he had disappeared. She woke up to find Travis sitting on her bed. She asked him why he was there. He said he had a dream about Josh. Josh asked Travis to follow him.

Travis started to follow, but Josh was going too fast. He had turned a corner to see Josh, but as soon as he reached him, he had disappeared, and he saw Megan crying. Megan told Travis about her dream. Travis asked Megan if she knew what it meant. Megan said that Josh wanted them to be together. Travis shook his head yes. They went to sleep with plans to get married at city hall.

The next morning, Megan, Travis, and Megan's dad went to city hall. An hour later, they were married. They called everyone and announced they were married. A month later, they were in Scotland at Travis's cottage. Everyone came out to see Megan and Travis. They looked so happy. Brandi thought to herself that they were meant to be.

CHAPTER TWELVE

The Kids

This chapter is different. It's about the kids and the grandkids. Brandi and Jeremy's kids, Wyatt and Draven, were what we will start with. Wyatt and Angel were very happy with their son Bradford. Wyatt was now twenty-five and Bradford was five. They all lived in Florida. Draven was directing a movie called, It's Me. It's about her life so far. She was engaged to James, Joe's son with Leann. They met at one of Draven's premieres. They fell in love instantly. James was now twenty-three. Zack and Sierra's twins, Angela and Angie, were now fifteen and have permits. Angie was a good driver. She was nice, pretty, and polite. Angela, on the other hand, was very crazy. She couldn't drive to save her life. She lost her virginity at thirteen.

Angela was in her room crying when Angie walked in. She asked what was wrong. Angela told her that she was pregnant. Angie asked who the father was. Angela told her she didn't know. There could be three possible fathers. Hank Good, Travis Lee, and Timmy Charlie. Angie asked Angela if she was going to tell Zack and Sierra. Angela replied with no. She was going to get an abortion. Angela went to the abortion center. The doctor said she had to have her parents' permission. She went home and told Sierra and Zack. Sierra wasn't upset but held her and asked who the father was. Angela responded with I don't know. Sierra asked her to go to the ones she thought were the fathers and tell them. Angela went to all three boys to tell them. They all agreed to take DNA tests when the baby was born. Nine months later, she gave birth to a girl and named her Diana Anne. All three boys were there to take a DNA test. Travis Lee was the father.

Travis was eighteen and went to Yale. He was nice-looking. Cole black hair, dark complexion, and dark eyes. Travis was happy to be a dad. He asked Angela if they could get married. Angela said that he had to ask her dad. Zack looked over to them, said give it a year, and then asked again.

Draven was sitting in the living room reading a romance book her mom, Brandi, wrote. James walked in and said, "Let's go to Las Vegas and get married. I don't want to wait anymore. I've lost all my family." Draven said OK and started packing. So that is part one of the kids.

CHAPTER THIRTEEN

The Final Kids

Angie was walking to work because her car broke down. She was walking down an alley on Thirty-Fourth. A hand grabbed her and threw her to the ground. He told her to keep quiet. He grabbed her purse and ran off. Angie got up and went to the police station. She told them what happened. They asked what he looked like. She couldn't tell them. They asked her if she had credit cards. She told them that she did. They told her that they would trace them and find him. A couple days later, the cops called and found the guy and arrested him. His name was Vinny Mcnally. Angie was relieved. A couple of weeks went by, and Angie was sitting on a bench in the park. A man stood by and asked if he could sit by her. She said yes. He told her his name was Tyler. They sat in silence for a minute. Then Tyler asked if she had got her credit card bills back yet. Angie asked, "What?" Tyler grabbed her and stuck a knife under her throat and cut her deep until she slumped to the ground. A couple of hours later, a couple found Angie's body. The cops showed up and called Sierra and Zack. Two days later, Vinny, a.k.a. Tyler, turned himself in. He got life without parole. They had Angie's funeral the day Vinny went to prison.

Draven and James decided not to have kids. The world was a horrible place.

Wyatt and Angel were still happy together.

Angela and her husband were still together and raising a very stubborn Diana.

CHAPTER FOURTEEN

The Car Wreck

It has been two years since the update on the kids of TBB. It's sad that some of the kids had passed away before their parents. Brandi was sitting in her bedroom when Jeremy walked in. By the look on his face, Brandi knew something was wrong. She asked what the problem was. Jeremy told her that he had to go to a meeting for his Alter Ego gig. They needed to make posters for the tour. He asked her if she wanted to go, but Brandi told him that she could not go because she was having Bette Midler over for tea. Jeremy walked over to her and kissed her goodbye. Jeremy brought up the time they first met. Megan and she were coming down the hall in the hotel in Las Vegas. He and Baby J, a.k.a. Josh, bumped into them. Brandi told him it was fate. Jeremy kissed her again and left.

Two hours later, there was a knock on the door. It was Bette Milder. They went down to the dining room. They drank tea and chatted for hours. It was three in the afternoon when Bette left.

Brandi went upstairs. Her phone rang. Brandi answered. It was Jeremy's agent, Brad. He asked if Jeremy was there. Brandi told him that Jeremy left hours ago. Brad told her that he had been at the meeting for eight hours and Jeremy hadn't shown up. There was a knock on the door. She told Brad that she would call back. She answered the door to find cops at the door. They told her that Jeremy died in a car wreck. She asked how. They told her that a truck was coming into his lane, and Jeremy swerved to the other lane to miss him. A car was in the other lane and hit him head-on. They asked her to come down and identify him. Brandi got into her car and followed them to the morgue. They pulled back the sheet. It was Jeremy. Brandi shook her head yes and ran out. She drove home. She just stood on the porch looking at the front door. She didn't know what to do.

Just then Sierra and Zack pulled up. They noticed that she looked a bit off. They got out of the car and asked her what was wrong. Brandi didn't respond for a bit. Sierra shook Brandi, and Brandi came to. She started crying. She stuttered her words to tell them what happened. Zack and Sierra covered their mouths in disbelief. Three days went by. Sierra and Zack had Jeremy cremated. They called everyone to come to Scotland to have Jeremy's ashes spread over the cliff. Everyone was on the cliff. Brandi was wearing a black dress down to her feet, a black veil over her head, and was barefoot. They spread the ashes and walked away to the house. Brandi stood there for an hour before leaving.

CHAPTER FIFTEEN

A Tribute to The Lost Boys Band Members

It had been two years since Jeremy passed away. In those two years, everyone decided to buy a house in Orlando, Florida. There were only five of them left, and they wanted to stay close together. Orlando was where it all began. Brandi was now forty-eight, Travis was fifty, Sierra was forty-three, Megan was forty-five, and Zack was fifty-seven. Travis and Zack decided to make a memorial for Jeremy, Joe, and Josh. They put a statue up in the middle of the park where they used to play basketball as kids. It was gray colored and had their names on it with their birthdays and death dates. They had a ceremony with fans, the mayor, and them. The news channels were there, and it was broadcasted on every major news outlet. ABC, NBC, and CBS. Members of other famous bands were there and performed songs by The Boys Band. Bette Midler was there and sang some sad songs. It was a wonderful tribute.

CHAPTER SIXTEEN

The Final Boys Band Member

It had been ten years since the tribute to The Lost Boys Band members. Zack was sixty-six years old now. Travis was sixty now. Megan was fifty-five. Sierra was fifty-three. Brandi was fifty-eight. Zack looked good still but has gray hair. Travis has gotten fat and bald. Sierra was a little chunky. She has long gray hair. She also had dentures. Megan had her red hair still. She was small. She was wearing glasses now. She looked younger than her age. Brandi looked good for her age. She still had blonde hair with a dash of silver. She wore glasses and dentures. She had lost a lot of weight since Jeremy died.

Zack was sitting in the study when Sierra came in. He asked her what was wrong. She told him that Brad called and wanted him and Travis to fly to Nashville to meet a new artist. Zack turned his head to look at his books on the shelf next to him. Sierra asked if he heard her. He said yes. He called Brad to make plans to fly out to Nashville.

Two hours later, they were all at the airport saying goodbye. Travis and Zack boarded the plane. Travis told Zack he had a bad feeling about this flight. Zack told him everything would be fine. The steward came by to ask what they wanted for dinner. They both chose chicken. They ate and settled back to rest. A big bang was heard and then expulsion. There was nothing left of the plane.

A couple hours later, the cops showed up at the house. Brandi answered. She yelled, "No!" when she saw the cops. The girls ran out and saw Brandi on the porch, crying into Officer Joe's arms. He told them that the plane crashed into another plane. There was nothing left. The girls decided to have the guys' names on the statue. That would be the funeral.

Two days later, they went to see the carving put on there. They didn't tell anyone about it. They just wanted to be the only ones there.

CHAPTER SEVENTEEN

Life After the Boys Band

Twenty years after the plane crashed, Brandi was now seventy-eight. Megan was seventy-five. Sierra was seventy-three. They still lived in the house in Orlando, Florida. The girls made a memorial holiday to honor The Boys Band. It was July 28. None of the girls remarried. They go to church every day. Every day, they did something the guys loved to do when they were alive. On Mondays, they did charity work like Zack liked to do. On Tuesdays, they went to basketball games like Travis used to do. On Wednesdays, they did night church service like Joe used to do. On Thursdays, they went to the theater like Jeremy used to do. On Fridays, they went to concerts like Josh used to do. On Saturdays, they went to the park and looked at the statue of the guys. On Sundays, they took Travis's boat out on the lake after church. The girls couldn't wait to see the guys again. They each wrote a book about their time with The Boys Band. All three books went number one on the best-sellers list. It stayed at number one for five years. That was the end of a true love story.

www.ingramcontent.com/pod-product-compliance
Lightning Source LLC
Chambersburg PA
CBHW020330180726
47991CB00019B/1125